GW00493267

YAKUP ALMILLER

...and the boy lost his faith in God!

Short Stories

NEWIDEABOOKS

First paperback edition October 2020

Publications Coordinator
Atakan Kelleci

Translator
Alvin Parmar

Book Cover Designer
Gonca Küçük

Graphics Designer
Meral Gök

And The Boy Lost His Faith in God / Yakup Almelek
ISBN (paperback) 978-1-8381587-1-2

Published by NEW IDEA BOOKS LTD
www.newideabooks.co.uk
info@newideabooks.co.uk
59 Edgecot Grove, Seven Sisters
LONDON   N15 5HE

NEW
IDEA
BOOKS

YAKUP ALMELEK

...and the boy lost his faith in God!

Short Stories

Translated from the Turkish
by Alvin Parmar

YAKUP ALMELEK

He was born in 1936 in Ankara. He completed his secondary education at Ankara TED College and his higher education at the Istanbul University, Faculty of Economics and Commerce. In 1967 he founded Almelek Printing Inks Paint Industry and Trade Co. which is still continuing its activities. In addition to his business life, he continued his cultural - arts and literature studies with great enthusiasm.

For many years, columnists have been published in various newspapers, especially Cumhuriyet and Şalom. The story "Beşlira" was filmed as a feature film and featured at the 42nd Antalya Golden Orange Film Festival.

In 2009, the New York Off Off Broadway titled "Business Man" was staged.

In 2010 he attended the "Awakening" New York Broadway Mint Theater.

In 2012, another author's "Blood Flood" was interpreted by the Abingdon Theater Players in New York.

Annie Ward is the director of the author's all the games on display in the USA.

The author's games, corner writings, stories and poems are translated into English, and Turkish and English editions are published in Arion Publishing.

Another play by the writer of "Collective Games" (Businessman, Blood Challenge, Awakening) came to the reader with the signature of "My Neighbor Richard Wagner" Mythos Dimension.

Since 2014, all books have been reissued, and they have been welcomed by literary lovers with high sales figures at the country's distinguished book fairs.

Yakup Almelek was awarded the "Ismet Küntay Theater Special Award" at 40th Ismet Küntay Theater Awards with "Awakening" which was played in "Gaming Band" in 2014-2015 season. In 2016, he founded Cultural Performing Arts by mobilizing its space and facilities with a brave, pioneering, young vision.

Yakup Almelek, a member of the PEN Club Turkey Center, continues his culture, art and theater studies.

Contents

...and the boy lost his faith in God!

He was six. He lived in a village surrounded by a forest. His father sold firewood to provide for the family. He would be starting school the next year. It was a sweltering July. All of his friends had gone away with their families for the summer. He was the only child left, with his father and stepmother.

He had lost his mother the year before when she was hit by a lorry. They had brought her to the house, injured. Three days later, his father told him that she was with God.

He was a strong boy... He was ready to start a war with God to rescue his mother – and he did not care how big God might be! If they ever met, he was going to shout right into God's face that He had no right to make orphans of children who love their mothers as much as he loved his mother. That was what he was going to do, come what may. And if God did not give him his mother back, he was going to go right up to Him and kick Him as hard as he could.

He was very good at kicking. Five or six months before, the neighbour's son had made fun of him because he was short, and he had given him such a good kick that the boy could not sit down for a week. He was going to do the same thing to God; he just had to find Him...

He left the house at about midday. His stepmother's friends were coming round to read each other's tea leaves.

She did not like him being in the house while she and her friends were telling each other's fortunes. He hated these women who kept coming over; none of them had been friends with his real mother.

He set off towards the forest. He really missed his mother. Maybe he would bump into God in the forest. Of course, ever since the day of the funeral, the neighbours had been telling him that God lived in the sky, but somehow this had never seemed particularly plausible to him. Of course, there was nothing stopping God from flying in the sky now and again, but how could it be possible for Him to spend all His time there? Even planes, after a certain length of time in the air, have to land, after all.

As he was walking, he looked at the pinecones at his feet. He would give the big ones a kick and watch how far they went.

Suddenly, a gunshot. He knew very well what they sounded like because his father would often go hunting. The sound of an animal screaming immediately after the shot made his blood run cold. He looked up towards the sky to where the noise had come from, and he saw something round like a ball falling to the earth. At first, he could not work out what it was. It struck the ground about thirty feet in front of him.

He ran up to it as fast as he could; it was a bird. His father had told him that these large birds were called "eagles". The poor thing was clearly injured. The bullet must have entered just under its right wing because there was a lot of blood there.

His eyes met the eagle's. It was not dead yet, but it could not have long left to live; fighting to keep its eyes open, it looked up at him with a desperate glance that seemed to be saying, "Help me!" He was surprised. What should he do? If only his mother had still been there... He could have asked her for help.

His father was not really the sort of person to reach out to those in need. If he had been, he would not have gone out shooting little birds and snow-white bunny rabbits, would he? His stepmother came to mind. She was not a warm-hearted person either. Was she going to leave her friends and her precious tea leaves just to tend to a wounded eagle? And if he told anyone else, he knew they would come, but would they not just shoot the eagle again then cook it and eat it?

He suddenly felt calmer after thinking about all that and looked at the bird again. It was having difficulty breathing.

Suddenly, the sound of a dog barking sent a shiver down his spine. It must belong to whoever shot the bird and must be looking for it. It would be here any minute; it was inevitable; that is what they had trained the dog for. And what would happen when the dog did get here? It would either kill the bird immediately, or else keep it from getting away and bark for its owner to come. He immediately stood in front of the eagle that was lying motionless on the ground and got ready to fight with the dog.

He had been right... The dog found them in a couple of minutes. It had burst out from between the trees, sniffing the ground. He recognised the dog immediately. It belonged to the cobbler from town. He had taken his mother's shoes to that shop many times. Every time he went, he would give the dog a sugar lump. And this huge hunting dog absolutely adored sugar lumps.

The dog recognised the boy immediately, too. As the dog was running straight towards him, he opened his arms as wide as he could, waited and gave the dog a huge hug.

"Look!" said the boy, kissing the dog, "This eagle is my friend. Don't you dare touch it! Go straight back to your master and tell him you couldn't find the eagle! If you'll do that for me, I promise you I'll bring you two sugar lumps everyday! Everyday!"

Just like every hunting dog, this dog was very intelligent. And he showed how much he liked this idea by barking and wagging his tail. Then he took a glance at the wounded eagle, turned round and ran off.

Now, the cobbler was a short, slow-walking man with a large belly from sitting on the same stool the whole day. His greatest pleasure was hunting. After a year of marriage, his wife had left him and ran off with their neighbour, the grocer. The pain almost destroyed him. But there was nothing that he could do about it, and ever since that day, his greatest pleasure had been to hunt birds.

He had joyfully told his dog, "Go and get it, boy!" The dog had set out like a flash and ran off in the direction he was pointing in... But after a long while, he had come back with nothing in his mouth. Surprised, the cobbler asked him, "What's wrong, boy? Where's the bird?"

The dog looked towards the way out of the forest. It was as if he was trying to get his master to go that way. But the cobbler did not know what to do. "Where the hell can that bird be?" he kept asking himself over and over again. Suddenly, he remembered something that he had read in the newspaper. It said that a few minutes before a large earthquake, animals start running this way and that as if they have gone mad. "Oh God, what do you know? There could be an earthquake here at any minute!" he muttered to himself. There was nothing he could do other than watch his dog running around panting for breath.

Meanwhile, the little boy knelt down next to the eagle and started to think about what he could do. Yes, now he remembered: one summer's day when he had been running in the garden, he had fallen flat on his face and cut his right knee. His mother had cleaned the cut thoroughly with a watery liquid and some cotton wool. After that, she had rubbed an ointment like butter into the cut with some more cotton wool.

He took the eagle in his lap and said, "Don't die, my eagle friend! I'm going to go and get some medicine, and then I'll make you better just like I learnt from my mum! Just, don't die on me! Wait for me!"

He looked at the eagle; it had tears in its eyes. The proud bird was crying! The boy started to cry, too. Their tears mingled.

The boy stroked the eagle, kissed its wings and neck and then ran home without stopping. His stepmother was still reading tea leaves with her friends... They did not notice that he was there.

He went inside the house; he took the bottle of the healing water, some cotton wool and some buttery ointment from the bathroom cabinet, as well as a bottle of water from the kitchen. Then he left without anyone inside seeing him!

He found the eagle just as he had left it, its chest rising and falling. He poured some water onto the wound. He could see the bullet in the eagle's flesh, so he pulled it out and threw it away. "Bad bullet!" he said, "Bad bullet, you wanted to kill my friend!"

He imagined his mother standing there next to him and smiled at her; she smiled back. "Will you help me?" he asked her. She kissed him on the cheek; he was happy. He had understood: with his mother's help, he was going to make his friend better. He rubbed the healing water over the wound with some cotton wool and waited a while; then he spread the ointment on some cloth and gently rubbed it into the wound too. Everything was going to be OK; it had to be OK: the eagle had become his new best friend!

He was not afraid because his mother was with him. He could not see her, but he could feel her. She must have got permission from God... either that, or she had escaped from God to help him and his new friend, the eagle!

As the eagle was his friend, there was no doubt that it counted as one of his mother's children. It made him happy to think that. His mother had two children now: the eagle and him.

He leant over the eagle and looked carefully into its eyes: there were no more tears on its cheek. So his friend had stopped crying; it knew it was going to get better. He hugged it and rubbed his cheek along its back. "Will you be my big sister?" he asked without expecting a reply.

It suddenly occurred to him that he had to go and find food. If he did not, how was his only sister supposed to survive? "I'll go and get you something to eat; wait here," he said and ran off as fast as he could. He sneaked in through the back door of the house without anyone seeing him. He took a few pieces of meat and some milk from the kitchen, crept out of the house and started running again until he was out of breath.

The eagle smiled when she saw him. Who says that animals do not smile or laugh? The eagle really was smiling at him.

He put the pieces of meat into the bird's beak and helped her swallow them. He poured the milk drop by drop into her mouth, too. They looked at each other lovingly.

The boy was worn out by now. He could hardly keep his eyes open. He put his thin little arms round his friend's neck, his head on her breast and fell into a deep sleep.

He dreamt about his mother; she was saying, "Well done, my little boy!" He was over the moon and woke up full of excitement...

Night was about to fall. If he was not home before it got dark, his father might get worried. He kissed his eagle friend on the neck a few times and ran home. As usual, no one paid any attention to him.

The next morning, he went out onto the street just after his father. He went to the grocer's, got some milk and set off for the forest. His friend was much better. She was trying to walk. They hugged each other.

He gave her some milk to drink. She was so happy she kept opening her beak, trying to tell him that she wanted more. "Wait," he said, "I'll bring you some more in the afternoon..."

Before long, they were playing games together. The eagle would fetch pinecones that the boy had thrown. The poor thing was still having difficulty walking, but because she liked the game, she managed to play.

Round about midday, when it started to get very hot under the trees, he went back home. He was in luck; his stepmother had gone to the shops. He put some cheese, meat, parsley and milk into a bag and went back to the forest.

His friend could walk around among the trees, albeit with a limp. However, the wound on her right wing had still not completely healed. The boy, like an experienced doctor, told her to lie down on the ground. The eagle understood and lay down on her left wing, just like an experienced patient.

The boy took the dressing off the wound and cleaned the area well with water. He put some more ointment on the raw area with some cotton wool and put a new dressing on the part that was bleeding. While he was doing all of this, the proud animal did not move a muscle. She had complete trust in this scrawny little six year-old boy!

When he had finished, the boy helped the eagle get up again. They started to walk together. The boy told her about where he lived, about his real mother and his father, and told her that he was afraid of his stepmother, too. The eagle listened to her young doctor carefully, but said nothing and just watched him with a wise look in her eyes.

The next three days went by in much the same way. Sometimes, the boy thought of the eagle as his big sister; sometimes, he just enjoyed her friendship.

He would bring food from home twice a day, in the hope that, along with the milk he brought from the grocer's everyday, his friend would be back to her old self as soon as possible.

The bond of love between the eagle and the boy was growing day by day; so much so that, whenever the boy went home, the eagle would miss him and remain staring at the path until he came back.

It was four days since the eagle had been shot. And now she was slowly beginning to find her old strength again. She even tried to fly again. She would take off and fly low for a few minutes before coming back down to earth.

On the fifth day, as it was beginning to get dark, and when the eagle had just come back from one of her short flight attempts, the boy explained a hope that had just occurred to him: "Listen, I really like you. I don't want to leave you. Take me with you to my mum. Please... My mum's at God's side and God lives in the sky. I could climb on your back and hold on tight. Maybe God's a good person, and he'll feel sorry for me and let me stay with my mum. And you can be her child to; you can stay with us!"

He waited for the eagle to reply. Because the eagle did not speak the same language as the boy, she could not say yes in words, but she told the boy that she would help him by stroking his face with her beak.

He was on top of the world. He was going to see his mother again, the person he missed more than anyone else in the whole world, and they were going to be a family again, together with the eagle.

When he went home that evening, he found his father waiting for him. "Come here!" said the man angrily. "I've just come back from the grocer's. He said you'd bought twelve pints of milk! What the hell did you do with all that milk in four days?" His stepmother was standing next to his father with a stern look on her face.

The boy went bright red. What could he say? He just stared at the ground in silence. His father walked up to him and gave him such a slap that it almost knocked him off his feet. But that was not enough for the man: he grabbed the boy by the ear and started yelling at him:

"What did you do with all that milk?"

The little boy could not take it anymore and blurted out, "I gave it to the eagle to drink..."

"You gave it to the Eagle, did you? You're making other children fat off my hard-earned money, are you? You stupid little bugger, I'll show you!"

The man started beating him from head to toe. Punching him, kicking him. If it had not been for his stepmother holding his father back, the boy would certainly have ended up crippled.

His stepmother yelled, "Are you out of your mind? Do you want to kill the child and get into trouble with the headman of the village? Do you want to go to court? I mean it's not like the headman isn't out to get you already! Go ahead, give him an excuse, why don't you?"

When his father heard the word "headman", he stopped. He had stood for headman, too, and that had lead to a falling-out between them. Even though such a long time had passed, the headman still hated the woodcutter...

He left the child. "Go to your room, you little shit! And tomorrow, you'll take me to the Eagle and I'll get his father to pay for all the milk he drank! Now, go to your room! Get out of my sight!"

He went and lay down on his bed; tears were streaming down his face and onto the quilt. But he was not crying from the pain. When his father was beating him, it had occurred to him that his father thought the eagle was another boy! In fact, there was someone in the village who everyone called the Eagle.

If he took his father to his friend, the real eagle, there was no doubt that he would shoot her. Maybe the eagle would make the first move and scratch out his father's eyes. Then it suddenly came to him: he would run away and never come back. His friend was more or less better. She could walk with a slight limp, and she could even fly. They would up and leave before his father could catch them.

Just then he heard the doorbell ring; his father's friends had arrived. In a bit, they would sit down to play cards. It would go on for hours, and sometimes huge arguments would break out. Then they would drink and pass out. They would sleep until midday the next day.

He fell into a deep sleep... In his dreams, his mother was wearing a pure white dress.

"Come darling, come here to me, that house is not for you," she was saying.

It was already light when he woke up. He got up immediately and went out into the courtyard in his bare feet. His father and his stepmother were snoring. There were two empty bottles on the table outside.

He got dressed straight away, put the leftover food from the kitchen into a paper bag and went out onto the street. Walking as fast as he could, he got to the place in the forest. His friend was not there; his heart started to beat more quickly. What was he going to do?

Suddenly, from above, from far above him, he heard a rustling sound. He looked up and saw his friend gliding in the air and coming towards him. Once the eagle had come and landed next to him, they hugged each other joyfully.

He told her all about what had gone on between him and his father. And he could tell that the eagle was very upset. He felt that the eagle was blaming herself because she had drunk the milk.

"Will you take me on your wings to my mum?" asked the boy. The eagle nodded her head. The child was over the moon.

"Well, let's go then. But first, we should visit the cobbler's dog and say goodbye to him... And I promised him I was going to bring him some sugar lumps. Look, here they are, in this paper bag."

They walked to the marketplace together. The eagle was not limping at all anymore. She was back to her enthusiastic self. There was no one around so early in the morning.

"And I'll tell you something else," said the boy to the large bird, stroking her head. "When my dad was beating me, my mum wanted to save me, but God wouldn't let her. She couldn't get away; she couldn't come to me. So I'm cross with God and I'm not going to talk to Him or even look at Him until He lets my mum go."

The bird nodded sagely, showing that she agreed with the boy. The boy continued, as if he had only just thought of it: "And if He still won't let her go, I'm going to kick him so hard he won't be able to sit down for a week!"

The boy looked at the bird and understood that she approved of his plan and he was very pleased.

As they were coming up to the cobbler's house, they could hear the dog barking for joy. The clever dog had sensed that his old friend had come to visit him with the eagle. He ran up to them excitedly. The boy opened his arms as wide as he could and gave the dog a big hug. He waved the bag of sugar lumps in the dog's face.

It was not normal to hear a dog barking at the crack of dawn around there. The cobbler's dog, in his excitement, had woken up quite a few of the people living nearby.

They worriedly opened their windows to see what was going on. And when they saw a huge eagle walking together with the woodcutter's son, they were struck dumb. And there was the cobbler's dog running around them, barking and jumping.

The boy noticed that everyone was looking at them. He proudly stroked his friend's head. "Let's go!" he said as he climbed onto the eagle's back, holding on to the thick long feathers, "Let's fly!" The eagle took to the air and they started to circle above the village.

The villagers were all very shocked to see this. They did not know what to say or do. This sort of extraordinary thing could only happen on TV, in children's films.

To get a better view, the people all piled out into the streets as they were. Some of them were even in their underwear.

The boy said, "Let's not be late or mum will be worried about us!" to the eagle.

At these words, the eagle flew higher and higher until she and the boy were just a dot in the sky. And then that dot, too, disappeared.

No one did anything that day. The boy and the eagle were the talk of the whole village. Those who had seen what happened kept telling the same thing over and over again. Those who had not lamented the fact and showered those who had with questions.

The cobbler explained that the boy must be a saint. Everyone agreed. The grocer said that he was not going to ask for any money for the milk, explaining in a very scientific way that anything you give to a saint is actually a donation

The headman announced that he was going to put a fountain up in the village square in memory of the boy and the eagle...

The boy's father filed for divorce on the grounds that since their wedding his wife had been treating his saintly son badly.

And the boy's stepmother decided to get her own back on the woodcutter for divorcing her by humiliating him whenever she got the chance, telling anyone who would listen that he had beaten a saint, even if that saint had happened to be his son.

The day that the boy walked around the village with the eagle was declared a public holiday by a unanimous decision of the Council of Village Elders.

For years, the villagers would look up into the sky between the clouds to see if they could find the boy and the eagle. They begged God for their return.

But no one ever saw them again.

A Jewish Boy

They lived in a two-storey wooden house in an area of Ankara called İstiklal Mahkemesi, a neighbourhood that opened onto Denizciler Street on one side and the famous Samanpazarı (Hay Market) on the other side. Most of the people who lived there were Jewish. That was why the few streets stretching from Atpazarı (the Horse Market) out towards Denizciler were known as the Jewish Quarter throughout the whole of the capital city.

A ten-foot or so stone corridor led to the wooden house. Immediately on the right, there was a squat toilet. In the out-building at the side, there were two small box-rooms. They counted as shelter for a woman and her two grown-up daughters. She had lost her husband while she was still young. The ground floor belonged to her uncle. Her uncle, his wife and their two small daughters squeezed themselves into two rooms. There was nothing else they could do. In those days, you were lucky if you had any kind of roof over your head.

The hero of our story lived with his mum, his dad, his big sister and his little brother on the top floor of this house that I have tried to sketch out in words. They appeared to be a fortunate family. I say that they appeared to be fortunate because outside the country a terrible war was raging in all its savagery. Fear had taken hold of every corner of the neighbourhood. Was war going to knock on their door and drag them too into a future of darkness?

The future held two concerns: the first was what could happen to the vast majority of people living in the country; the other one, the uncertainty in which a small minority found itself regardless of what could happen to the vast majority.

Humanity was being wiped out beyond Turkey's borders in that godforsaken war that lasted from 1939 until 1945.

Was 1939 an inauspicious year? Maybe it was. Ten years before, 1929 had – economically speaking – jolted the world, first and foremost the United States of America, and all but brought it to the brink of bankruptcy. Between 1929 and 1939, principally Germany but also Japan and Italy set about rearming as fast as they could. North America and Russia, along with many other countries, were keeping a close eye on Germany especially, but without lifting a finger.

Armament results in war. That is how it was yesterday, that is how it is today, and if our world should have the good fortune of having a tomorrow, that is how it will be then, too. Armament ends in tears.

However much the five-person family which lived on the top floor of the wooden house could perceive happiness through their good intentions that is how happy they were. The father worked non-stop from morning to evening as an accountant in one of Ankara's famous bookshops at a tempo that would even have made the bees jealous. "Thank God," he would always say, "I'll never get rich on my salary, but I can support my family without them having to rely on anyone else, and that's enough for me."

"That's enough for me" or "that's enough for us" – these were the father's philosophy of life. This principle never made him wealthy, but it never reduced him to the level of never being grateful with his lot.

Naturally, the mother knew the family's finances very well. She managed the salary that her husband would hand over to her at the end of each month so well that her three children never went without the calories and vitamins that they needed to grow up big and strong.

In 1936, a big wooden box turned up in the house. The children immediately learned that it was called a "radio" and fell in love with this strange contraption. The first day that it was turned on, a carnival atmosphere filled the wooden house. A good-natured sprite had climbed inside the box, and he was the one who was doing the talking. As for the music that it would play, well, it was performed by a troupe of another sprite's little helpers, a good-tempered, sweet-faced sprite who liked humans very much. Or at least, as the children had not yet started primary school, that was their explanation. The father would tell them that magnetic waves travelled between the transmitter and the receiver and that was what radio was until he was blue in the face: the children paid no attention to him because they still had that gift of seeing everything in their own colourful world through the prism of their imaginations.

One bright spark – who had only just recently learnt to speak himself – got it into his head that he would climb into the box and sing too. Another little mischief-maker was afraid of getting too close to the box and would look at from ten feet away or so with a scared look in his eyes.

The neighbourhood had all read about the invention of a machine called a "radio" in the papers, but they had not had the opportunity to size it up with their own eyes or to hear it with their own ears. When they heard that the father had bought one of these magical boxes, they all ran to the house and shook their heads sagely, wondering what other wonders they would witness in their lives. They bemoaned not having got their hands on one of these talking boxes for themselves before the father had. Wives laid down the law to their husbands saying that they too wanted a box for the house just the same as this one.

The four-cornered box had four buttons: on-off, long wave, medium wave, short wave. On long wave, the father would listen to Ankara Radio; on short wave, a station broadcasting in French. Because the short-wave signal was weak, the father would turn the volume up to almost full-blast. And this would bring complaints from the mother and the children.

Twanging vibrations like singing or talking did not use to disturb their youngest child, who could only have been about one at that time, at all. Whether he slept or not had no relationship with anything that came from the outside world. Whenever his metabolism required it, and without paying any attention to what was happening around him, he would lie down on the bed flat on his back, shut his eyes and within a few seconds he would have floated off into the embrace of who knows what beautiful dreams.

His brother, who was four years older than him, was another matter:

"Dad, I can't sleep, can you turn the radio off, pleeeease?"

To which the father would reply that he could not, and that he would just have to get used to sleeping to the sound of the radio.

Then the boy would moan that he could not sleep to the sound of the radio.

So his father would tell him that it was his own fault if he could not sleep and that he should just try to learn to live with it. And this reply was always a reason for a row to begin between mother and father:

- For pity's sake, it's five in the morning! Who listens to the radio at the crack of dawn anyway? And you're listening to it at full volume! You could at least turn it down!

The father would be listening to a French broadcast. Ankara State Radio's Turkish broadcasts started later.

- You can't turn the short-wave volume down on this radio! Anyway, I'm listening to world news. It's important what's going on in the world, and anyway, why do you think I bought the damn thing in the first place if I wasn't going to listen to it?

- It's not like you have to listen to the news on the radio; I mean, you read the paper every day, isn't that enough?

- No, it isn't. And even if it was, this is my one pleasure in life. Morning, noon and night I'm wearing myself out with books and order letters – listening to the radio is how I relax, OK? Can you understand that?

- And you still haven't told me how much money you paid for this new toy of yours! Just so we can save some money, I don't hire anyone to help out in the house. Don't you think it wears me out, three kids, the laundry, the ironing, the cleaning, the cooking?

One of those standard domestic rows.

How had the radio come to the wooden house? Here is how: a shrewd businessman was so impressed by this brand spanking new invention that he had seen somewhere in Europe that he somehow or other managed to get all the necessary stamps and paperwork to import it into the country. This wooden or plywood box crossed the border into the country and reached the capital. The father bought this magical device - whose existence he had heard about in the bookshop - with the money that he had managed to scrimp and save. He would always boast to his wife that all the person who brought the radio to Turkey had to do was to wave his hand, and he would have found one hundred customers, but he had chosen him: he had sold it to him!

The radio was instrumental in introducing the Jewish Quarter to the outside world in those days.

In September 1939, the Nazi armies attacked Poland. In the same year, they occupied Denmark and Norway. Would Russia just stand back and do nothing? The time was ripe; the month was auspicious; they entered Finland.

While two children who must have been about three or four years old were playing catch on the street with a ball the size of a tennis ball that they had made themselves out of rags, a smart car that they had not seen until that day pulled up on the near side of the grocer's just ahead of them. They both immediately stopped playing and went up to the car.

One of them asked the person who got out of the car if it was his. The man liked the boy's bright eyes and good manners and told him that it was not, but that he was the chauffeur.

Then the child asked if they could look at the car. Of course they could, the chauffeur said. The two children joyfully went up to the car, and the other one asked if they could look through the window. The chauffeur told them that they could, but that they should be careful not to get their hands dirty on the car. The two boys craned their necks in wonder to look inside the car, keeping their hands behind their backs.

Then one of them asked the chauffeur if he drove the car everyday. When the chauffeur told them that he did, the blond-haired boy asked if they could get inside the car and sit down in it – just so that they would be able to see it a little better.

The chauffeur told them that they could but that first they should go and scrub their hands and faces so that they would not make the seats dirty. The children gladly agreed and told him that they would be back straight away and that he should wait for them. The chauffeur told them to be quick.

The blond-haired boy invited the other boy to get washed at his house, but the other boy did not want to because the blond-haired boy's mother would get angry. However, the blond-haired boy reassured his friend that his mother was not there because she had gone to visit his grandparents, so they both ran over to the house and were out of breath by the time they arrived.

They washed their hands and arms and even – to get the sand out of it – their hair with well-diluted soft soap. They returned as fast as their legs could carry them. They found the chauffeur chatting to the grocer.

"We're back!" said one of them, "Look, our hands and arms are clean; we even washed our hair!" The chauffeur took a look at their hands, arms and hair and told them that they could get in.

The chauffeur opened the front door for them, and the two children got in the car with excited, proud looks on their faces.

The chauffeur, seeing that they looked like good kids, decided to make their day and offered to take them for a ride round the block. The blond boy could not stop imagining how wonderful it would be, and the other one, as if in a dream, muttered to himself, hardly able to believe that he would be going for a ride in that beautiful car.

The chauffeur took them round the neighbourhood for four or five minutes. Until then, there had scarcely been a car of that or any other model that had ever entered the neighbourhood. It created quite a stir, a brand new, luxury motor going round the streets. The children in the street ran after the car. When they saw their two friends sitting in the front seat, they shouted out to the driver to let them have a ride too.

The chauffeur pulled up in front of the grocer's where he had picked the children up. They got out.

Suddenly, as many as ten children appeared running up to the car. They looked at it in amazement and awe. The chauffeur said good-bye to Osman, the grocer, and drove off.

They showered the two children with questions. Even the grocer enjoyed listening to what the little scamps were saying among themselves.

The blond-haired boy went home after an hour. He told his mum that he was not hungry. And the poor, worn-out woman did not insist. The boy washed his feet, put on his pyjamas and went to bed without waiting to be told off. He fell asleep as soon as his head touched the pillow. In his dreams, he was back in that car. He was at the wheel and it was definitely somewhere in heaven. He was driving down a leafy lane. When the road came to an end, he noticed that the car had turned into a boat, and now he was in the sea, travelling across the ocean blue. Finally, the sea, too, came to an end, and the car became an aeroplane. It was flying above cottony white clouds. He was visiting countries that he had heard about in his geography lessons.

When his mum came into the room, she could tell he was dreaming from the smile on his face. She looked at her son lovingly for a few minutes, leant over and kissed him on the cheek. So as not to make any noise, she tiptoed out of the room and closed the door softly behind her.

The other boy left his friends and went home, too. His father was listening to the radio as always. His little brother was sleeping, snoring ever so lightly, and his sister – because she had started primary school now – was doing her home-work. His mother was in the kitchen.

He was so excited that he could not eat a mouthful. He could not get the car ride out of his mind. He lay down and forced himself to think. Would he own a car like that when he grew up? Or else, like his father said, would the war wipe everyone out?

He promised himself that he was going to work very hard and do whatever he could to save up enough money to buy the same kind of car. He thought that if only he knew what the owner of the car did for a living, then he could do the same and have a car of his own one day, too. He fell into a deep sleep, contemplating the scene he had summoned up before his eyes.

After a while, his mother came into the bedroom. When she saw that her son had got into bed without getting un-dressed and was sleeping soundly, she felt happy. She gently took off his shoes, socks, shorts and t-shirt and dressed him in his pyjamas. She kissed him on both cheeks, then tiptoed out of the room and closed the door softly behind her.

In their bedroom, her husband had dozed off listening to the news on the radio. She knew full well that her husband was going to get up at five and breathlessly listen to the latest, mainly disastrous, developments in Europe on French radio.

The threshold of war was drawing closer. She put on her nightie and went to the window, looked out between the curtains at the dark clouds in the sky and thought to herself, God, don't let me live to see my children die, let me die before them!

Her husband had started snoring. Did she love him? She thought so. She was just hurt that he had not told her where he had got the radio from or how much he had paid for it. She smiled to herself and wondered how heartless she must be if her man kept such a small secret from her.

Thinking this made her feel a little more relaxed. She got into bed and fell asleep listening to her husband breathing as if it were a piece of music.

The owner of the car called his chauffeur. There was something rude and harsh in his voice. "Yes, boss?" said the chauffeur gingerly.

- Don't call me boss! I'm not your boss!

- Well, how should I address you, then?

- You can call me sir. I find it suits me rather better.

- Very good, boss. Oh, I beg your pardon, Sir.

- Good, and I liked the "I beg your pardon," when you say it, it sounds refined, you know, like how cultured people talk.

- I shall pay attention to that when I speak, boss, I beg your pardon, Sir.

- Now tell me, what did you do with the car yesterday?

- After I dropped you off at your friend's house, I stopped off at the grocer's to buy some cigarettes, and then I went home.

- You took two kids round the block for a drive, didn't you?

- Two kids? Ah, yes, I remember now; they were both about five and I took them for a little ride.

- Did you know that those two boys were Jews?

- Well, that never even crossed my mind! You mean those two little kids were Jews?

- Yes, my dear chauffeur, you took two Jewish boys for a ride in my car. Do you know what the Jews are like?

- Well, we live in Balat in Istanbul. Most of the people who live there are Jewish. After my father passed away, my mother became good friends with our Jewish neighbours. They get together twice a week to play cards. I think it's a game called cooncan.

- Now, wait a moment, my dear chauffeur. Don't you go sticking up for them! Do you know what they're doing to the Jews in Germany?

- No, Sir, what are they doing?

- The Germans have banned them from working and they're not allowed to leave their own neighbourhoods.

- I see, but why? What have they done wrong?

- What have they done wrong? How am I supposed to know what they've done wrong? Hitler doesn't like them. Isn't that enough?

- But, Sir, where did you hear this from?

- Where did I hear it from? My nephew's a student in Münich and he wrote to me about it.

- Well, Sir, I don't know anything about the Jews in Germany, but we've been living in the same neighbourhood as Jews for sixty years in Balat – my mother, my father and some of my relatives. And we haven't seen anything bad about them. Maybe a few were no good, but...

- Well, well, well, so now you're standing up for the Yids! You should know you're station! But it's my own fault:

I should have known better than to try and talk to you, you just disagree with everything I say. Go and wash the car, we're going out in an hour.

The chauffeur left, angrily, without even looking at his boss.

Later that day at Osman Efendi's grocery shop, the chauffeur came in:

- Hello, Osman.

- Hello there! Why the long face? Is something wrong?

- Yes, there is. I'm leaving my job.

- Leaving your job? What? But why?

- My boss needs his head examined! You know how I took those two kids for a ride in the car yesterday? Well, he got angry about that. Not cause I took them for a spin, but because they were Jews. The man's gone mad, I'm telling you! How can you work for someone like that?

- Why did you leave Istanbul to come here? Isn't there any work over there?

- I was a driver there, too. Instead of being a taxi driver, I thought I'd find a comfortable position somewhere as a chauffeur. I saw in the job ads in the paper that this bloke was looking for a chauffeur. And what do you know? His advert went in the Istanbul column instead of the Ankara column by mistake. Anyway, I wrote him a letter straight away, and he answered it, and here I am in the capital.

- I'm not being funny, but is he paying you well?

- Very. About twice as much as I could get in Istanbul. Everything's cheaper here than over there, and I've even been able to save.

- Well, that's good. Anyway, are you married or single?

- Single. My dad passed away six months ago. My mum had a bit of money put away, but still, I wanted to come to Ankara to work and save a bit, y'know, buy a place for my mum and one for us.

- Who's us?

- I'm engaged; we're planning to get married next year. We don't want to live at my mum's. And anyway, she doesn't want us to either. A place for her and a place for us.

- You don't want to live at your mum's, I think you're right. Your wife would never survive your mother nagging her. I've been through it and I wouldn't wish it on my worst enemy!

- But what am I going to do now? How am I supposed to work for that madman?

- Now, I'll be your honorary uncle seeing you've got no father anymore, so, nephew, you look like a clever lad. How old are you and what's your education like?

- I'm twenty-four. I finished middle school. But when my dad got sick, I stopped going.

- Anyway, what difference would it have made if you had stayed at school? We see what happens to people who stay on. Driving is a good job, better than staying at school and becoming a civil servant!

- You're a man of the world, what do you think I should do?

- Well, if you want my advice, listen up. But of course it's up to you if you take it or not.

- I'm all ears; I could use all the advice you can give me.

- Well listen up then and answer me this.

- Ask away.

- What should you do to the hand you can't bite?

- Kiss it?

- That's right, well done. You've passed the first test with flying colours. I'm afraid you've just got to kiss his hand, this man whose chauffeur you are. Only until you're strong enough to bite it, mind! Once you're strong enough, you can bite it, crush it, do whatever you want.

- I see.

- And I've seen your boss. And his wife and two daughters. His wife's ugly as sin, and his two little girls are fat. The whole family's fat and overweight.

- When did you see them?

- The week they moved in. Look, nephew, I'm a grocer! If anyone moves in to the area, we start doing our homework straight away. Who are they exactly, do they like their food? What about fruit and veg?

- Well, I can see I'm going to learn a lot from you! It's so you'll be able to understand if they'll be your customers, isn't it?

- Exactly. Now, listen, here's what we're going to do now. Whenever they send you out to buy something, you come to me, OK? Buy whatever they want from me.

- Of course I will! I'm not going to go to anyone else: you are my honorary uncle, after all.

- I'll give you ten percent of anything they buy.

- What do you mean? I don't understand.

- What's there not to understand? Let's say you buy something for three lira, I'll give you ten percent. So, come on, what's ten percent of three lira?

- Well, it's thirty kuruş.

- And there you go: I'll give you thirty kuruş.

- Are you really going to do that?

- Of course I am! I'm not talking out of my hat now, am I!

- But you'll be losing money, then… Why are you going to be giving me ten percent of your money? That money's rightfully yours.

- Rightfully yours too because you'll have brought me custom.

- But maybe my boss will come by himself and become your customer in his own right.

- He's been living here for a whole week now and he still hasn't come. He sends you to the shop round the corner.

- Wow, so you know that, too! But what if he finds out?

- Don't worry, he's not going to find out. It's just between the two of us, you and me. And mind you don't go telling anyone, don't even let on to your best friend.

- Do you think I don't know how to keep my mouth shut? But, wait, what if he buys ten lira's worth of stuff a week, does that mean you're going to give me one lira?

- With pleasure!

- Well, I don't know what to say. I'll be rich! And the first thing I'll do is buy my old dear a flat. She'll be over the moon, over the moon.

- You're a good lad. You'll go straight to heaven if you think about your mum and help her out. That's what the hodja said before Friday prayers.

- But I can't stop wondering: if you give me that money, you'll have less, you'll be earning less.

- Don't you go worrying your pretty little head about that. I know what I'm doing.

- But what? Come on, Uncle Osman, you can tell me.

- You think I was born yesterday? Me, give you my trade secrets?

- Come on, Uncle Osman, it's not like I'm going to be telling anyone.

- Oh well, why not, I've taken a shine to you. Ok, listen, I'm going to overcharge your boss by ten or fifteen percent. Or else, I'll give him short weight. Let's say you want four pounds of tomatoes, I'll give you three and a half.

- Ah, now I see!

- There's another variation on the theme: I'll weigh whatever he buys in thick brown paper. The brown paper itself is a couple of ounces.

- Does this go on in all corner shops?

- Some do, some don't. It depends on the customer.

- Some customers must be very generous, then. They don't look at the scales, don't ask the price, don't try to bargain.

- An experienced shopkeeper knows what kind of customer he's dealing with just by looking at him.

- But what if my boss or his wife send me to the shop round the corner, not to you? We've been doing the shopping there for the past week anyway.

- You'll work on them, slowly, slowly. Tell them something like you've compared prices and it's more expensive there, or the produce isn't very good there.

- OK, then, I will.

- God will help you because your motives are good. You want to buy your mum a house and then one for yourself and your intended.

- Do you have any children?

- Four. The two eldest are boys and the others are girls. I've bought each of them a house. I wouldn't wish rented accommodation on my worst enemy! You take it from me, you need a house so you won't have to keep listening to the landlord always nagging you.

- You're right. I've got enough trouble putting up with my boss. Anyway, I should be going now; I've got to take the boss to the barber's.

- You work with that man. I've heard on the grapevine he's a black-marketeer and a real nasty piece of work. He's got very rich, too. It's no sin to cheat someone like that.

- Thank you, you've opened my eyes. Here, let me shake you by the hand!

- Yes, let's shake. God bless!

In the Jewish Quarter, the appearance of this magic box that carried electromagnetic waves scattering words and tones from a transmitter to a lot of receivers was an event in itself. Even though the news was censored, Turkey could still find out what was happening in other countries with this incredibly useful system they called radio.

Before the Second World War broke out, news from Germany that secretly reached Ankara revealed the existence of a serious altercation between German Christians and German Jews.

Also, French radio was saying in veiled tones that hundreds of Jews from Berlin had left Germany. Jews who lived in Frankfurt, Munich and Düsseldorf were watching events in Berlin very closely.

What had made the German Christians suddenly change their minds over the last twenty years about these people who had been living in Germany ever since it was founded, a people who shared past and future, heart and soul with them?

The father was looking for an answer to this question.

Then, one day something very exciting happened to him.

A German customer came into the bookshop. The shop assistant could not speak any languages, so he called the father from the accounts office. The customer was in his sixties with hair that was just starting to go grey.

He wanted to have a French book sent over to Ankara from Paris within twenty days. The father assured him that if they telegraphed the order, there should be enough time. The customer was overjoyed and muttered something to himself in German.

The father, who was taken rather unawares by this, asked the customer if he was Jewish. The man bristled. Trying to keep his anger within the bounds of politeness, he said that he was German, but that if he was only being asked what his religion was, then he was a Christian, but that he was proud to be able to count many Jews as friends.

Years later, as the father was telling his children this story, he would tell them that the customer had been right to get upset: nationality and religion are not the same thing.

That day, as he was sipping a cup of Turkish coffee that the father had ordered for him, he started to tell his story:

- I'm professor of sociology at the University of Berlin. I've been arrested twice for criticising Hitler and his SS. They had to let me go for lack of evidence. My old students in the Ministry of Foreign Affairs advised me to escape while I still had the chance. I'm going to go to America from here.

- Well, why did you come to Turkey then, asked the father hesitantly.

- Turkey is neutral! It's safer than any of the European countries!

- Oh, if only you'd stay here, you could teach at Ankara University.

- How did you guess that was what I was really thinking of? That's actually why I'm here. I've applied to the ministry and I'm just waiting to hear back from them, smiled the German professor.

The father thought that his German guest might be able to rid him of his curiosity about the Jews; after all, a couple of minutes ago had he not said that he had many Jewish friends? Gathering together all the moral courage that he could, he asked what the situation of the Jews living in Germany was like.

- Very, very bad. Terrible. I read in a letter from a friend today that they've started to arrest Jewish professors on trumped-up charges and take them away nobody knows where to.

- But why? What for?

- Why? Are you really that curious?

- Do please tell me!

- Hitler was one of the founders of the National Socialist German Workers' Party. They won the 1930 elections. Ever since it was founded, they've been attacked by various institutions, but especially Jewish professors. In time, quite a few famous Christian professors started to jump on the bandwagon too. These movements were supported by some Jewish businessmen.

The German professor paused for a moment to drink some water and the father stepped in:

- Is that why Hitler hates the Jews?

- If only it was! If only that was all there was to it! Hitler needed to find a scapegoat. In the thirties, the German economy was very bad. The Wall Street Crash in 1929 had huge effects on almost every country in Europe. In those years, in Germany, there were seven million unemployed. Hitler pinned the blame for it on the Jewish minority. In almost all of his speeches, he would make the accusation that Jewish companies were the reason for the high unemployment. In any other year, people would have laughed at him. No one would have believed him, but unfortunately, Hitler managed to deceive a part of the German people with his evil genius and rabble-rousing rhetorical skills. Those who saw through him kept quiet, burying their heads in the sand. And those who wouldn't keep quiet were removed from the scene by Hitler's SS. Most of them were killed.

- Didn't the Jews defend themselves?

The professor smiled bitterly. He was pleased that the father was taking such an interest.

- At first, the Jews didn't pay any attention; they said that the Germans were not stupid enough to believe such cock-and-bull stories. There were even some who, unfortunately, ridiculed Hitler. But eventually Hitler's power surprised them and crushed them. Young Germans did not pay attention to their arguments. No one listened to them; no one even read what they wrote in the papers...

- You said something about young Germans, what was their role?

- Well, Hitler made much of the fact that the Germans were a superior race and that other countries had to serve them, and he got his cronies to do the same thing too. Germans were Aryans, the master race. Jews, blacks and homosexuals had to be eliminated. That was the message: destroy them!

With trembling voice, the father asked:

- How can thinking minds be taken in by something like that?

- It's easy to misdirect the young; rousing speeches work very well. Germany lost the First World War. The country had an inferiority complex. Energising society and encouraging it was just what the doctor ordered. Hitler saw this and took advantage. Young people in Germany today have got to the point where they are very hard-working, self-confident and where they'd gladly throw themselves into the fire if it meant Germany would win. They obey the Führer's every order without thinking twice. That's what it's like today.

\- Well, the war continues, but is Germany going to win?

\- No, it's impossible because just military, or even economic, power is not enough to win a war. They have to propagate a culture that the people in the lands that they have occupied can accept, too; they have to keep them happy, but what are German soldiers doing? First, they shoot Jews, blacks and homosexuals on the street in front of everyone, and then they attack whichever woman take their fancy. The streets are filled with terror.

\- How can there be a happy ending?

The professor smiled:

\- I like that phrase, "happy ending". Here's how there can be a happy ending: first, the people in the occupied lands will revolt and start a guerrilla war. The Germans cannot fight a guerrilla war. They will get harsher, they'll carry out more atrocities, and resistance and terror against them will increase. In the end, they will be overcome and have to leave those countries.

Second, Hitler, drunk with victory, will attack America and that's when the happy ending will come. We stand no chance against an America ready to support England tooth and nail. Not even one in a hundred.

Third, Hitler's going to be egged on by his sycophants and declare war against Russia and what happened to Napoleon is going to happen to us, Germany, too. Our army will be smashed and we'll have to turn back...

The German professor stopped; it was clear how upset he was. Then he said slowly, "Germany is going to lose the war, and we will hang our heads in shame for years to come."

Ever since the beginning of the conversation, the father had been wondering about the professor's family. Did he have any children? Where was his wife? It might have seemed out of place or even rude to ask, but in the end he could not stop himself and gingerly asked the professor if his family had stayed behind in Germany.

Sorrow appeared on the his mature face:

- Unfortunately, we lost our nineteen-year old son in the War. In spite of all his mother's best efforts to stop him, he volunteered for the army, along with hundreds of other young people. He was shot during the occupation of Paris. And I lost my wife three months ago. She fell ill, and, who knows, maybe it was because of her grief, but it had carried her into the Unknown within a month.

The father wanted to change the subject.

- But you're on the winning side; someone else would have been proud of what's happening, but you criticise your country, and you've been arrested twice for it. It's very noble!

The professor stared into the father's face, their eyes met and both of them faintly smiled.

- We're on the winning side today; tomorrow, we're going to be on the losing side. Our backs will be bent under the weight of the shame that all our barbarity and cruelty has brought us. I can never approve of what is being done to the Jews. They are just as German as I am. I'm just as German as they are. And as for homosexuals, call it whatever you want, a life choice or a disorder, no one has the right to look down on them, let alone kill them! And one more thing, why did we set out to occupy Europe? We chose a group of leaders with mental problems, and we're following them. No country can enter another country by force! What are we? Barbarians?

The father listened spellbound to the German professor. It was as if he was giving a lecture to his students at university. It must have been for his fiery, not to mention right and humanistic speeches that he had been arrested twice. He spoke so sweetly... The father wanted him to keep speaking so that he could keep listening.

Then it suddenly occurred to him that he should perhaps invite the professor over for tea on Sunday afternoon. His wife would like that. Osman the grocer would give them top quality salami, sausage, olives, jam and cheese. He could pay at the beginning of the month when he got paid; that would not be a problem.

Of course, it would be a huge expense for them, but to invite maybe a world-famous German thinker to their house would be an honour. That was real wealth. It was worth all that money just to be able to listen to someone like that.

Then he suddenly remembered: the house. His house was not nice. It was small. It was certainly immaculate, but is was not the sort of house which you could show a guest round with pride. And suddenly he saw it again. The toilet. They only had the one toilet. Eleven people had to use the same toilet. What if their guest suddenly had to use the toilet and one of the children was using it at that time and left it dirty! What if his wife did not have enough time to clean it…

He could not take the risk. He preferred to let his wife know and decide once she had said it was ok. He so wanted to be able to invite this man to his house!

- What are we? Barbarians? We cannot hold someone's skin colour or religion against them! We don't have the right! No country should be under the illusion that it has such a right, and if it is then we are no better than savages!

The professor stopped and drank the water that was left in the glass in front of him.

- Is that the time, my dear friend? I should be going now. If you'd like, I'll give you a deposit for the book I've ordered.

The father told him that that would not be necessary, and that as soon as the book arrived he would let him know and that he could pay for it then. The professor wrote down the address of where he was staying on a piece of paper.

After they had shaken hands and as the professor was leaving the shop, it struck the father that the professor had a happy look in his eyes.

That day, the father left work a little earlier than usual so that he could take the German professor's order telegraph to the post office himself.

As he walked, his head was filled with pleasing thoughts. He would tell his wife what the professor had said. Including him calling him "my dear friend" as he left. He had never thought of himself as particularly dear or valuable; on the contrary, he was only one of the millions of nondescript people who lived on the earth.

He had lost his father when he was ten years old. There was no possibility that his widowed mother would be able to send him along with his two brothers to school. After primary school he did not go to middle school, even though he really wanted to, so he taught himself instead: he had started learning French when he was at the Jewish primary school, and he managed to get it up to a very good level by himself. And maybe it was only by the grace of God that he had managed to find a job in a bookshop.

He would always have his head in a book. Turkish and French literature, he was familiar with both.

As he entered the post office he sighed to himself, "Once my children have grown up, I'll tell them what the German professor said. It's important they know about the Second World War and what happened to the Jews. They've got to think about how Turkey behaved. My kids should not live like vegetables with no idea about the world.

His mother was fuming and telling him off. "I'm sick, sore and tired of you! If you're not making your little brother cry, then you're stopping your big sister doing her homework! Go out, get out of my sight!"

She was always like that whenever visitors were coming. She did have a good side. She definitely never raised her hand against her children. In fact, she had never even as much as laid a finger on them. She would just yell at them whenever they did something naughty. Yet how many times he had seen other mothers giving their children a terrible thrashing? His mum was definitely one of the best mums in the world.

What did being naughty mean anyway? It was difficult for a five or six-year old child to understand. It seemed to him that whatever he did it fell into the category of being naughty. The best thing was for him to go out onto the street. It was neither the time nor the place to think about things like that.

Just as he was closing the door behind him, he heard his mother telling him to come back when he heard the hodja giving his sermon from the minaret.

In those days, children did not have watches, so the hodja's call to prayer from the minaret of the Hay Market mosque would define noon, mid-afternoon and evening for them.

He asked his mother what was for lunch. His mother replied in a sad tone of voice: "What else have we got? Beans and rice." Of course he knew his mum was going to say that, but still he told her that he was bored of beans, rice or chickpeas everyday. "I'm not going to eat them! I want meat!"

He had learnt this tactic from his big sister. Whenever she was angry with her mother, she would keep shouting how much she hated beans and chickpeas. He went out without noticing the tears of frustration in his mother's eyes, the frustration that she could not give her children what they wanted to eat.

In the Ankara of those days, you could find everything but only if you could pay the black market rates, of course.

Who had enough money to give what the conmen and war profiteers were asking? Very few.

Being able to give three children what they wanted, things like meat or chocolate, was not a luxury that a father working in a shop on a normal wage could afford. Even bread was rationed. Each child was entitled to two slices per meal. Often mothers and fathers would share out their own slices between their children.

That was how war was. You would not wish it on your worst enemy.

That day, if only the mother had found a little time doing the housework and turned the dial of the talking box. She would have been happy to learn that the German army had attacked the USSR. It was June 1941.

She would have been happy because everyone was expecting Germany to enter Turkey, as friend or foe. Attacking Russia might mean that they were not thinking of attacking Turkey after all. There was a rumour going round that when the German generals suggested invading Turkey to Hitler, he is supposed to have said that it would be possible to go in, but not to stay because the Turks are ferocious against foreign forces.

Another rumour was this: the German army's Russian campaign started at 03:15 on the morning of 22nd June. Of course, intelligence services all over the world informed their headquarters of this immediately. The news reached the Foreign Office in Ankara. They had to tell President İnönü. It was the middle of the night; how were they going to waken up İnönü, who almost every night would go to bed well after midnight? They asked Mevhibe İnönü, the first lady, to do it. She woke him up and gave him the news. İsmet İnönü was, apparently, so happy to hear it that he leapt out of bed and started singing to himself and dancing.

Where did the father say he had heard this from? His children could not remember.

The value that our president, who was famous for being dignified and cool-headed, put on this piece of news showed this: by attacking Russia, Hitler had sown the seeds of his own destruction.

The boy who had gone out onto the street because he had been told off by his mother knew absolutely nothing about all of this. He was living his life taking advantage of all the blessings of being five years old. After eating, he would lose himself in games with his friends. When he came home, he would fight with his little brother. All of this would make him so tired that as soon as he sat down at the table, he would wolf down whatever was set down in front of him without even noticing that it was beans and rice, which he claimed not to like.

As he was walking along, he kicked a pebble that he liked the look of with his right shoe and followed where it went with his eyes. He bumped into a friend:

- Hey, if you kick stones, you'll ruin your shoes! Yesterday night my dad gave me a beating because of that.

- Why are you going to ruin your shoes if you kick a few stones?

- Look, the leather on the toe of the shoe comes away from the sole. If you kick stones, it slowly starts to come away.

- So what?

- What do you think, clever clogs? They'll let water in when it rains.

- So what? Water's not going to do you any harm, and it'll soon dry.

- Yeah, but your socks'll get wet, won't they?

- I don't wear socks in the summer.

- But what about the winter, clever clogs?

- By the time winter comes, these shoes will be too small for me and they'll give them to my little brother.

- You're lucky, first you wear them and then, once you've worn them out, you give them to your little brother.

- What happens in your family?

- First my big brother wears them, and when they're too small for him, they give them to me.

- Don't wear them, then.

- But then my mum gives me a good hiding.

- My mum never hits me.

- Sometimes it's my mum that beats me, sometimes it's my dad.

- That's terrible! It'd be better if just one of them beat you!

- Like I said, clever clogs, you're lucky!

- But what does that mean, lucky?

His friend thought for a while and expounded wisely: "If you're only beaten by your mum, or only beaten by your dad, then you're lucky."

- Ha, I see. So that's why I'm lucky.

- Yes, you're lucky.

- Why do you keep calling me clever clogs?

His friend thought for a moment:

- You know our neighbour's daughter, Sara? Well, she always says clever clogs, and that's why I say it.

- Has she started school yet?

- Yes, she's a big girl.

- My big sister's started school too, but she never says clever clogs.

- Why not?

- How do I know? I'd better ask my dad.

- How'll your dad know?

- My dad knows everything.

- Why?

- Because he reads a lot, he's always reading.

- Why?

- Because he wants to know everything.

- My dad doesn't read books; he reads the paper.

- The paper might be good too.

- Hmm, if my dad gives money for a paper everyday, it must be a good thing.

- Do you want to play marbles? I've got loads in my pocket.

- I can't. My mum's waiting; she'll thump me if I'm late.

- Why are you so scared of her? I'm off.

The boy went on his way, kicking any pebbles that he could see. He was well aware that he was not going to bump into any of his other friends this early in the morning, but what could he do? If he went back home, the chances of him getting a good telling off were so high. Rather than run that risk, it seemed more sensible to wander round the silent streets.

He started when he saw a big, burly boy swaggering up towards him. He could tell that something bad was going to happen, so the best thing was just to pretend he had not seen him. He knew that that boy was the local bully. If he started teasing him, he would not answer. The boy was big but like most fat kids he was definitely weak...

He crossed the road and started to pretend he was looking at something else. He could feel his heart racing. It went through his mind that he should have stayed at home and that his mum yelling at him was definitely better than this. But there was nothing to be done now. Maybe the fat boy would go on his way without bothering him.

But his worst fears came true. The fat boy did not go on his way. There was evidently something that was annoying him, too, and he wanted to take it out on something. When they got level with each other, the fat boy yelled over:

"Oy, you, you Jew!"

The thin boy was surprised. He had not been expecting something like that. What could the local bully mean by calling him a Jew? He had to come up with an answer immediately; otherwise, it would mean that he had lost. Or would it be better to pretend he had not heard and to carry on walking? No, he was not a chicken, was he? Only a chicken would try and run away from a fight. Anyway, maybe there would not even be a fight; they would just yell at each other and the whole spat would be over in minutes. Suddenly something came to mind that he liked. He raised his voice:

"Oy, you, you're the Jew!"

Oy, you... He was happy as those words came out of his mouth because they showed self-confidence and there was something in it that was insulting to his opponent. But what on earth did Jew mean? Why had he called him a Jew? Being a Jew definitely could not be something good! From now on, if anyone called him a Jew, he was going to answer in the same way. Served him right, he had got even. He had got his own back...

So, now it was the fat boy who was surprised. What was he supposed to do now? If only he knew what *Jew* meant. He had heard his dad angrily saying "bleeding Jew" a few times about someone from work. So being a Jew was something that made the other person angry. He could make this thin kid who he had only just met angry like that. He already had made him angry... He tried again.

"Jew, Jew, you're a Jew!"

He sang these words to the tune of a well-known song. He had not planned it like that. It had come to him spontaneously. When he saw how effective it was, he was happy again.

The thin kid was quick to reply. He used the same style. He just made one minor change: he sang "Jew, Jew, you're a Jew!" to the same melody, but jumping up and down. He started to repeat it.

This really annoyed the fat kid. Adapting annoying words to a song was his trademark. And here was this scrawny kid who had stolen his invention and was using it against him shamelessly. And doing the Charleston to it was just another sign of his disrespect.

Things had gone too far. He could not let him get away with it. He was not going to have his own invention used against him.

The two boys walked towards each other. The fat boy hit the thin one in the face with all his might. The thin boy reeled. But he was not intimidated. He tried out something he had seen in *The Revenge of Les Pardaillan* and tried to damage his opponent as much as possible.

They were both out of their minds with anger.

It was obvious that the fat kid was more experienced in one-on-one fights, but he got tired out quickly because he was overweight. He grabbed the thin kid by the waist and tried to wrestle him to the ground. He managed and so did not have to worry about getting kicked anymore. They both fell onto the soft earth. They both had a good hold of each other and were rolling about on the ground.

And it was in exactly those few minutes that the black-marketeer's official car, with the chauffeur from Istanbul, Osman the grocer's honorary nephew, behind the wheel, turned into the street. The chauffeur was not a particularly curious person, but when he saw what he originally thought were two tramps fighting with no holds barred, he felt he could not just let them get on with it and go on his way.

He stopped the car and got out.

"Stop! Stop! What are you fighting for?"

The chauffeur's appearance on the scene ought to be remembered with love by the two boys because it was why the earnest desire for someone to come and break them up hatched in their unconscious minds. Most people in a fight have this secret desire. They prefer to have a neutral third party get involved and share the honours by coming to an agreement with words rather than fists or weapons.

Even though they were only five or six, this is what the two boys wanted too. They did not have to know why. They had no doubt about it: they did not want to injure each other. They did not even know each other. They were just naively coming up with their own version of the behaviour of people their fathers' ages. Would it not be good if someone came and broke them up!

The chauffeur's firm manner stopped the two boys. They loosened their grip at the same time. They separated their arms.

The chauffeur would not let it lie and asked why they had been fighting.

Suddenly he seemed to remember the thin boy. He could not be one of the two Jewish boys that he had taken for a ride in his car the week before, could he? He looked the boy up and down carefully and asked him if he was the one he had taken for a spin.

The boy took a certain pride in having been recognised and said, "Yes, Mr Chauffeur, and I had a friend with me."

The chauffeur remembered how well-behaved the two children who he had taken for a ride in his car the week before had been. He had been sent away with a flea in his ear because of them. It would not do for him to let up. So, the thin one was Jewish, but he had never seen the other one before. He must have been from a different neighbourhood.

He asked them why they had been fighting, in a nagging tone of voice.

The thin one bravely pointed to the other one and said, "He called me a Jew!"

The other one would not let him gain the upper hand and immediately reacted. "But, mister, he said I was a Jew, too!"

The thin one felt that he had to look stronger in the eyes of the chauffeur. "But I swear, he said it first, mister, I swear on the Holy Qur'an, he said it first!"

The chauffeur began to laugh. "But look, son, that's a Muslim oath. Don't use it."

The two boys were surprised. Why should they not use it? It must have been because he already knew the chauffeur and for some reason that he could not explain liked him that the scrawny boy gathered together his strength and said, "But everyone uses it. There's a woman who comes to our house to help my mum; she's always saying it."

The young man, who was in the position of being both teacher and, for having broken up their fight, rescuer to the two boys, had understood the situation: the fat boy was Muslim and the thin one was Jewish. He thought back to the Jewish families who had been his neighbours in Balat for years. He looked the two scamps up and down once more and turned to the Jewish one and said, "When you want to make an oath, you have to say "on the Torah".

The boys definitely did not understand this. They were hearing the word *Torah* for the first time. What was the thin child supposed to do? He was embarrassed to ask what this new word meant. So he just replied like a good boy saying, "Alright, next time I'll say that," and that made both him and the chauffeur happy.

It did cross the other boy's mind why the scrawny kid should have to say "on the Torah" instead of "on the Holy Qur'an". He was embarrassed to ask the chauffeur too because when he asked his dad anything, often his dad would scold him, telling him that it was something that he would not be able to understand, but that he would understand it when he was older.

When can you say that a child is "older"? While that was one of the things about which he was the most curious, he had thought it through and come up with this hypothesis: when you start school, you are "older". He was counting the days until he would enter the stone building at the top of the street wearing his smart school uniform. He would learn everything there and he would not have to ask anyone anything else ever again.

Grown-ups know everything about everything, and they are always, always, always right.

So being grown-up was a good thing. Knowing everything, like his uncles did.

The chauffeur said to the two rascals, who were ready to listen to him, "Look, kids, fighting is bad, and it's wicked. Now you're going to make peace and you'll never raise a hand to each other ever again. OK? Do you promise?"

At the same time, they both gave a sincere, "Promise, mister!"

Author's note: Twenty-five years after the radio, was television not received into our homes with a similar interest?

Saving the Ship's Honour!

In the port of Haifa, a Turkish passenger ship was getting ready for the Haifa – Cyprus – Istanbul sailing. It was to set sail at two o'clock that morning.

Towards midnight, three people boarded the ship: an Englishman in his thirties, athletic, quite tall and fairly handsome, and two young American women. They were both about twenty-five, both of medium height, one of them was dark-haired and the other, fair-haired, and both of them were pretty enough to catch a man's eye.

All three of them were carrying backpacks. It was clear that they were students who were more than likely making the most of their youth by travelling the world.

They climbed up the steps from the harbour and, when they got to the third-class deck, put down their heavy rucksacks with a sigh of relief. As they were taking in their surroundings with big smiles on their faces, the ship's steward suddenly appeared. He looked the three of them over carefully, half in mockery, half as if he was trying to hide the fact that he himself would not have minded being like them.

He was a young man, too, barely thirty, if that. He was short and plumpish. He had a typical Black Sea appearance with his thick hair, moustache and well-trimmed beard. He could have tickled the fancy of many a European woman.

His English amounted to about two dozen words. He took this opportunity to use some of them with pride:

"I'm your steward for the voyage. May I see your tickets, please?"

The Englishman nodded and smiled, and took out the carefully folded ticket from his back pocket and handed it to the steward. After the steward had spent some time examining the ticket, he opened his eyes wide and said:

"This ticket is for three women or three men, not for two women and one man." He then tried to hand the ticket back to the Englishman with the satisfaction of knowing that he had done his job well.

The three foreigners were surprised. The Englishman did not take the ticket back; the dark-haired girl had some harsh words for the steward. He could not understand what she was saying so just repeated what he had already told them.

The situation was getting tenser and tenser. And now the fair-haired girl entered the fray. She leaned over and picked up her rucksack and motioned for her friends to do the same; the other two picked up their rucksacks as well and headed for where the cabins were. The steward, wanting to give the impression that it would take more than this to scare him off, got in front of them and puffed up his chest to block their way.

The Englishman pushed the steward to one side to make a path for himself and the two girls. The steward realised that he was not going to be able to get the better of three people on his own, so he deftly grabbed the dark-haired girl's bag, ran as fast as he could to the railings overlooking the sea and stopped. The Englishman and the two American girls went after him at the same breakneck speed. The steward lifted the bag above his head, threatening to throw it into the sea if they came any closer.

The three of them immediately understood the gravity of the situation and stopped. They shouted across to each other, trying to make themselves understood, but it was no help to either side.

During this enforced cease-fire, another passenger came on board. He was a twenty-five year old student called Yalçın... As he was coming up the stairs, he heard the noise. Smelling the tension in the air, he immediately came between both sides and told them in English and Turkish that he was willing to act as a go-between.

These two short sentences created somewhat of a thaw among the four. The scowls melted away. In the first step towards reconciliation, the steward politely gave the bag back to the dark-haired girl. He offered her four more of the English words that he knew: "I am very sorry!"

Was this gesture perhaps what kindled the fire of love between the pretty, dark-haired American and the young Turkish man?

Yalçın asked the steward what the misunderstanding was all about.

- They've got a ticket for three, but they're not married; I mean, the man isn't married to any of the girls.

- How do you know?

- You can see it straight away. And even if you can't, it says so on the ticket: they've all got different surnames.

- Do they have to be married to share the same cabin?

- Of course they do, this isn't some kind of knocking shop! It's a ship! An important place!

- Well, let me ask them now.

He turned to the foreigners and told them in English, "He says you can't stay in the same cabin because you're not married."

"What?" said the dark-haired girl, "It's none of his business if we're married or not!"

The steward butted in and said to Yalçın, "I understood what she said. A single girl and a single man cannot stay in the same room. We're not just going to turn a blind eye to something like that!"

"God!" the dark-haired girl fumed, "Can this country really be so backward? What century are you living in?"

This was too much for Yalçın, "Hey!" he replied, "Wait a minute! I was in Boston last month. In the boarding house where I was staying they told me I couldn't bring any girls to my room. Not even as a visitor. What century are they living in over there?"

- "That's different. This is a tourist place."

- "But it's the same mentality. Anyway, now's not the time to be arguing about it!"

Yalçın turned to the steward and asked, "So what happens now?"

"The ship's half empty; they can take another cabin. The two girls can stay in one and the man can stay in the other," the steward suggested.

Yalçın translated the steward's suggestion for the group. "But that's impossible!" said the Englishman, "We don't have enough money to do that. But let's say we did take another cabin, is that steward going to be watching over us night and day? He's never going to know if one of the girls sneaks into my room."

Yalçın translated what the Englishman had said into Turkish.

"That's quite true, and besides, we're under strict instructions from the captain not to interfere with anything like that. What they do is their own business," said the steward.

Yalçın exploded, "Is that how it is? I've never heard such a load of two-faced nonsense in all my life! It's all a charade!"

"What are you arguing about?" asked the dark-haired girl, "We bought our ticket from Turkish Maritime Lines' Haifa office. Why didn't they tell us then? And the person who sold us the ticket was Turkish, too."

The steward piped up, "I understood what she said. We're not bound by any mistakes the agent might have made. If they don't have enough money to take another cabin, they should get off the ship."

But Yalçın pointed out that that was not a decision the steward was entitled to make. "They say they haven't got enough money, and I'm sure they're telling the truth. And what would be so terrible about the three of them sharing the same room, anyway?"

- "Don't you know anything! Didn't they teach you about the birds and the bees at school? A ship has honour, don't you see? Honour!"

YAKUP ALMELEK • 65

- "What? And you're here to defend it, are you? Anyway, a ship isn't a living thing. A person can have honour, yes, but a ship? You have people from all over the world coming on a ship, and every passenger's honour is his own business. Everyone's responsible for themselves."

- "Oh really?"

- "And the company that sold the ticket was Turkish, for God's sake! Don't you think they'd have some idea about what honour is? Or are you the world authority?"

- "OK, OK, there's no need to get angry! Anyway, like I say, the captain doesn't really bother about that sort of thing. I'll show them to their cabin. Oh, and if it's not too much trouble, can you ask them if they smoke and if they could give me a few packs. I'm flat broke."

After lunch the next day, the Englishman and the two American girls told Yalçın that they would like to speak to the captain. Yalçın was curious about what they might want to talk to the captain about. But he knew that it would not be appropriate for him to ask a foreigner that sort of question.

Yalçın told the steward what they wanted and asked him to make an appointment for them with the Captain. Now it was the steward's turn to be curious:

"I wonder why they want to see the Captain? They're not going to complain about what happened yesterday, are they?"

He started to beg Yalçın: "Yalçın, I'll do anything, just don't let them say anything about me to the Captain. What happened yesterday is all water under the bridge!"

Yalçın tried telling the steward that they were definitely not going to be telling tales to the Captain about him and that he should not worry, but to no avail. In fact, the steward was right to be worried. Three months earlier, something vaguely similar had happened. A German tourist, a woman, had complained about him to the Captain. Apparently he had been looking at her, a single woman, with a little more than the usual stewardly concern. The Captain had given him a dressing down in front of the German tourist and told him that if there were ever any more complaints, he would be fired without getting a certificate of good conduct.

"I won't be able to send money back home! My family will be out on the streets! My wife and kids will starve!" He was practically in tears. Yalçın was his only hope. If Yalçın could make it clear that it had all been just a misunderstanding and that it had not been the steward's fault, the Captain might not give it much thought.

Although they had only known Yalçın for one day, the three tourists had grown very fond of him and wanted to be friends with him.

The steward was pleased about that, too. That way, Yalçın would be able to hear whatever they said to the Captain for himself.

Also, it would be wrong to say that Yalçın was not interested in the dark-haired American girl. Her large eyes, the energy in her laugh and her fine figure were not things that could easily be ignored...

Yalçın told the steward, "Don't worry! There's no real chance of that happening, but if they should complain about you, I'll do whatever I can to try and make sure you keep your job. But now go and get us an appointment with the Captain."

The steward froze for a few minutes. The Captain would see them on the bridge in two hours' time.

Back on deck, while they were lying in the sun, chatting, to pass the time until their appointment with the Captain, the steward suddenly appeared with a tray. He had brought them tea and biscuits. It was obvious that he was looking for some way to apologise for what had happened the day before.

The dark-haired girl reached for her purse, but he told in a mixture of Turkish and English that it was a gift and that he would not accept any money.

This was the tactic he probably always used to win over foreign passengers.

At exactly four o'clock they were on the bridge. The Captain was a broad-shouldered, robust man of medium height. He must have been in his fifties. His greying hair suited his white uniform well.

"Well, how can I help you?" he said as he shook everyone's hand in turn. His English was pretty good.

The girls looked at the Englishman. When the young man had gulped slightly and plucked up enough courage, he said, "Sir, I am English and these girls are American. We're all students, and we're travelling round all the important and beautiful places in the world. We got to know each other in Haifa, completely by chance. And before getting on this ship, we stayed in together in the same hotel room for ten days because it was cheaper that way. And during that time, we understood…" and here he pointed to the fair-haired girl, "that we love each other, and, when we get back home, we're going to get married."

The Captain was listening carefully. He had taken a shine to these three young people.

"Sir, my girlfriend is against us being together outside of marriage. I respect her beliefs. So for this reason, we would like you to preside at our engagement. As Captain you are the father of the ship, and, as such, we ask this of you."

The Captain frowned slightly. He was a father, too, and felt that he had to offer the best solution to these three young people who had asked for his help. He asked, "Do your families know about this? Of course, you're old enough to make your own decisions, and you don't need to ask them for permission, but it would be more considerate at least to let them know."

They answered in unison: "We've written a letter; it's in the cabin. We're going to post them from Cyprus."

Now, this answer did not entirely satisfy the Captain. He continued, "It'll take a long time for the letters to reach your families. Wouldn't it be better to call them? And I know what you're going to say. It's expensive to call. Well, why don't you phone from the ship? I don't want any money from you."

This made them happy. They thanked him and wrote down their phone numbers on the piece of paper the Captain had handed them.

First, the Captain called the number that the fair-haired girl had given him on his radiophone. A woman answered, and he said, "I'm the Captain of the ship that your daughter is on, and I'm passing you over to her."

Her mother was very happy. When she heard what her daughter had to say, she showed her support by saying, "That's great, honey! If he's good enough for you, he's good enough for us. We can't wait to meet him. I'll tell your father the good news just as soon as he gets home from work."

It was clear that the girl had an excellent relationship with her parents and that both sides trusted each other.

Then the Captain called the number that the young Englishman had given him. The English are known for their phlegmatic nature and it was possible to hear it in the voice thousands of miles away on the other end of the line.

"Really? Well, I'm very pleased for you. Of course, you'll be bringing her over; I'll get your room ready. Your father's gone for a walk – it's his day off today. We'd have preferred you to marry someone English, but if you've set your heart on her, it must mean there are good Americans, too."

The two American girls burst out laughing at that last sentence.

The three young people waited respectfully for the Captain's decision like schoolchildren in front of a strict but fair schoolmaster.

The Captain was satisfied.

"You both love each other, and your families are not against you getting married. I shall oversee your engagement. Now, where are the rings?"

The fair-haired girl's joy was clear in her voice:

"The ship stops in Cyprus tomorrow for five hours, Sir. We're going to buy them then."

The Captain thought for a couple of moments and gave his reply:

"Tomorrow evening, after we have left Cyprus, I'll be having a cocktail party with the first-class passengers. I shall announce your engagement then and present you with your rings.

The three young people thanked the Captain, who with a few words had made them so happy, leapt to their feet and hugged him as they would have hugged their own fathers.

The Captain, maybe remembering his own children, who were more than likely many days away as he was at sea, said, "You can go for now, but come back in an hour. I'm inviting you to dine with me tonight. The First Mate will be there too."

Yalçın was secretly proud that he had also been invited, even though he was not directly involved.

As they were going back to their cabins, they found the steward fidgeting, waiting for them nervously.

"Well, what happened? What happened?"

Yalçın had told him that the Englishman was getting engaged to the fair-haired girl, and the steward want to know everything right down to the tiniest details.

The steward was jumping for joy.

He looked up to the sky and struck his foot on the ground three times:

"Thank you, God, the ship's honour has been saved once more!" he shouted.

Five Lira a Week...

It was about half a century ago, but still, this story has lost none of its vividness for me and I think of it as one of the defining moments of my life.

It was 1946 or 1947. I was ten or eleven. We were still living in the house where I was born in Ankara. The Second World War has just finished. Europe was busy licking her wounds. Turkey, fortunately for us, had managed to stay out of the War thanks to the clever politicking of her statesmen. Even if Turkey was exhausted, she could look towards a secure future. Throughout the land, people were talking of democracy. The Democratic Party had been founded...

What was the greatest pleasure that a ten-year old boy could have in those days? Of course, it changed from boy to boy. Mine was going to the cinema. However, I had a serious problem: money. I could only watch a film once every two or three weeks. The cinema was in Kızılay in Ankara... How much I loved that cinema! So much so, that for me, it seemed like heaven's Ankara branch. It was far away from where we lived. Two or three kilometres there and back. It did not matter. It did not even seem difficult to get there. It was a pleasure.

I had two other friends who were as mad about the cinema as I was. We would save up all our pocket money, collecting every penny that passed through our hands as if it were a valuable work of art. Then, when the time came, we would make the six-kilometre round trip to watch a never-ending film, something like the thirty-six part *Les Pardaillan*. Coming back was also fun. We would tell our friends who had not gone all about it and tell them how wonderful it was. Often we had to tell the same story several times as a friend would ask to hear what we had seen again and again.

One day, after we three chums had spent a happy time in the cinema, something caught our attention: the audience all left through one door. One of us thought out loud whether it would not be possible to sneak in through that door when the guard was not looking, taking advantage of the hustle and bustle at the end of a showing? There was only one security guard at the exit. And he was a complete oaf as far as we were concerned. Dead from the neck up.

Should we give it a go? Why not? We all immediately agreed. We took our places the next week. As the audience was leaving from the exit, we three heroes sneaked in like three spirits. The man on the door did not have a clue! It was a fantastic success. We congratulated each other on our own cleverness. Five or six days later we tried it again, and we got to watch another film for free. We were becoming experts! Now, we would no longer have to spend our pocket money on the cinema. We could blow two weeks pocket money on one of those really expensive Princess cakes from Akalın patisserie.

They say third time lucky. With us, though, it was the exact opposite: our third attempt ended in what I can only call a fiasco. And what a fiasco it was! The man on the door, the one we had thought was asleep on his feet, saw us as we were trying to sneak in. He reared up with the violence of a mare who has had a cigarette stubbed out on her rump. "You little bastards!" he roared. There was no way he was going to be able to catch all three of us. But he did catch one of us. He started punching and kicking our comrade in arms. I can still hear my friend pleading, "I won't do it again, sir! Please don't hit me!" ringing in my ears. He was only saved by bystanders stepping in. The three of us went crying to the chemist. His cuts were patched up. Then we went home.

That evening, my father, without even looking at me, said, "If you like going to the cinema so much, go and work somewhere until school starts again. You can spend what you earn however you want." In those days, going against what your father said was something that did not bear thinking about, and expressing your own opinion was like breaking a taboo. So, like it or not, that Monday I started work.

They call your first love your "first eye ache". The first eye ache of my work life was an oil and soap wholesalers. It was somewhere that my father thought would be suitable for me. My job was not really that difficult. In the morning, I would give the floor a good sweeping and dust the shelves. But the most important thing was to keep the sacks of soap and tins of oil spotlessly clean, especially the tins. I would wipe them so well that you could see your own reflection in them. That was when I first encountered what we called "Arab soap": the famous brands like Persil and Tursil were not available in Turkey back then. The tins of oil had to gleam. If a tin was dusty or dirty, the customers would have said that it had gone rancid without even looking at it, let alone tasting it. As for the sacks of soap, we wanted to sell them as quickly as possible because – if I remember correctly – the longer they stayed the shop, the more they dried out, and the more they dried out, the lighter they became. And as they were sold by the kilogramme, I did not want less money to go in the till or less profit to be made.

Finally, my first week was over. I was really curious about how much I was going to get paid. At noon on the Saturday, five minutes before closing time, my boss called me in. "Listen," he said, "I'm pleased with you. You sweep the floors well, the shelves are clean, the sacks and tins are well kept. I'm going to give you five lira a week."

God be praised! Had I heard correctly? Five lira! That was a whole five hundred kuruş! Was it possible? I could go to the cinema twice with that money! And by bus, too! I could even have one of those expensive Princess cakes! And a glass of pop! Not to mention a dish of pistachios and almonds!

Those days are etched in my mind. Who was I then? A ten-year old boy. The answer is correct but lacking. I was a giant among boys. You may think that that is all a load of hot air, but I was earning exactly five hundred kuruş a week: what was the difference between me and Aristotle Onassis or Vehbi Koç? Think about it.

On that unforgettable Saturday, I was so excited I could barely stammer out a thank you as I took the money from my boss. I dashed out of the shop. A neighbour spotted me and told my father. Holding the money in my left hand and waving it in the air, shouting "Five Lira a week! Five Lira a week!"

There we have it. Since then, I have not cared for any kind of reward that has not been the fruit of my own efforts.

Sometimes, as I am leaving a cinema, I remember those days. And my eyes mist up with memories.

Damned Money!

As Kezban was taking items of her husband's underwear one by one out of the washing basin in front of her, wringing them out and rinsing them, she was muttering to herself, "Damned money, damned money!"

Why was she so angry?

She had been married for fifteen years. She had four children. They could have had more, but a curse had descended on their lives. A curse that had put an end to their happiness.

Her husband had inherited a piece of land in town from his father. Because a road was going to be built very close to where the plot of land was, it had suddenly multiplied in value. Kezban's husband had sold the plot and then, the first thing he did was to pay a rather hefty dowry for a slip of a girl from the neighbouring village and take her as his second wife.

All hell broke lose.

One day when her husband was out, Kezban gave the second wife a damned good hiding. The second wife did not hesitate to complain, making everything seem three times as bad as it was. Because of this, her husband beat her – his wife of fifteen years – in front of the children. The children, all of them between eight and fourteen years old, did not speak to him for six months.

Where was that old domestic bliss?

Although Kezban had only gone to primary school, she was very clever and liked to think things out for herself.

As far as she was concerned, if her husband had not got rich by selling the plot of land, he would not have been able to take a second wife. So it was money that was mostly to blame.

The root cause of her unhappiness was money.

Money was like a train taking the world somewhere bad, according to Kezban...

God had not created Satan. People had invented money, and then turned it into the devil.

Money was the devil; the devil was money.

Money was just something vile that deceived people. Whoever had it thought they were far better than they actually were and ended up doing all kinds of foolish things that they would never have done otherwise. Or at least that is how Kezban saw it...

Love of money was different to any other kind of love. You could love your mother and father, your husband or wife, your family, your friends, or you could love playing the fiddle, but love of money was something more powerful than all of these. It took them all over and could not be overcome. This was Kezban's philosophy of life.

But in the end, what was Kezban to do? She bore responsibility for the family on her shoulders and in the end, like it or not, she made peace with the second wife. The two women got along as sisters. Harmony reigned in the house once more.

Kezban had thought all the possible details through well and wrote notes in a primary-school exercise book that she had taken from her son. Then she got the notes to the village teacher, a man who had lost his wife.

Whenever she had time after doing the housework, she would write. She even tried her hand at poetry. The teacher took a lot of interest in her. He would even visit her from time to time. And Kezban always kept a careful eye on him. Sometimes they would meet in secret.

The second wife knew all about it, but pretended not to.

The Sorrow of Adam and Eve

Millions of years ago, the earth was without form; it was only a dark ball of gas.

And the Exalted Creator of the universe said, Let there be light: and there was light. And He divided the light from the darkness and night and day were born. He called them day.

And God saw that it was good.

And He formed the oceans from the gases and the sky. And this was the second day.

And on the third day, the Greatest Power said, Let the waters be gathered together into one place, and let the dry land appear. And it was so. The continents appeared, and trees, fruit, plains and meadows appeared on the face of the earth.

And on the fourth day, the sun, the moon and the stars were created. Seasons, days and years came into being.

And on the fifth day, fish filled the waters of the seas and fowl filled the air.

But there was still more to be done. On the sixth day, the other animals appeared on earth. Man was God's most beloved creation.

And on the seventh day, the Great Architect of the Cosmos looked at all He had done. And He saw that everything was perfect and eternal, and He rested.

God told his two-legged creatures that they should work for six days, but that the seventh is a day of rest. This command has been obeyed to the letter. People have chosen Friday, Saturday or Sunday as a holiday, depending on their beliefs.

On the sixth day, God created Adam before Eve. Why? Because the land needs to be worked; it has to be tended. Every man's first duty is to work the land at the beginning.

So our forefather, Adam, set to work in a garden full of beauties that words cannot express, but he was not happy. He was lonely; he had no companion. Who could he talk to? Who could he share his thoughts with?

God saw this and created Eve from Adam's rib.

Adam and Eve liked each other very much.

Eve fell in love with her man's wiry neck, thick hair, deep looks and muscular body. And Adam was smitten as soon as he saw Eve's long hair, pencil eyebrows, her thin eyelashes, her rosy cheeks and her figure that he just could not take his eyes off.

Love is as blind then as it is now... So much so that Eve, in spite of God expressly forbidding it, could not resist the fruit of the tree of knowledge, ate from it and offered it to Adam, her beloved.

Fruit: when offered, it is not refused; it is taken...

God was angry that they had not listened to His word, so he drove them out of the Garden of Eden. Now, Adam and Eve were all alone. Around them, there were no creatures like them. What could they do besides being there for each other?

As time went on, Eve's stomach began to grow. In those early years of their lives, when they were still young, how could they have known what getting pregnant was? They were both very afraid... What was happening to her body?

They thought of asking God, but they were afraid. God was angry with them... They had eaten the forbidden fruit and had been driven out of the eternal realm.

As Eve went into labour, they started worrying even more. And after nine months and ten days, they watched in astonishment as a baby emerged from its mother. They had seen similar things in some of the four-legged animals, but it would never have occurred to them that the same thing could happen to Eve.

When the baby opened its eyes onto our world and when it cried much more loudly than its small size would have led them to expect, they did not know what to do. Thinking it was hungry, they stuffed plants and meat into its mouth. When it stopped moving, they left it and went on their way.

Eve was soon back to her old self and gambolling hand in hand and frolicking with Adam.

After a while, Eve's stomach began to grow again. It did not make them afraid like the last time, but it made them upset. They had not liked that little creature at all. Was the same kind of thing going to be coming?

It was. Adam held the baby up by the feet and showed it to Eve, "Look," he said, "it looks just like you."

They liked this second one no better than the first. As well as its crying, it couldn't even go under a tree and go to the toilet like all the animal babies in the forest did. And it smelt so bad that mother and father had to hold their noses, and in the end, they offered it to the wild eagles as food.

In four years, a third baby also lost its life in similar circumstances.

The angels who had seen what had been happening went and complained to God. If things carried on in the same way, the human race would become extinct after Adam and Eve. Something had to be done.

God held a meeting about it with all His angels and helpers and issued a decree. This decree was proclaimed from the seventh heaven and throughout the cosmos. It said this: "From now on, all babies are to learn to be happy, to smile, to laugh from the moment of birth."

Eve was not particularly bothered by her fourth pregnancy. When the baby was born, Adam left it on Eve's arms. The little thing pressed its head against its mother's breast with an unexpected energy and started to drink. Adam and Eve were surprised.

When the baby was full, it started giggling and waving its arms and legs around in delight. Its favourite thing of all was to pull its father's hair. The sounds it made to show that it was happy, were the sweetest thing you could ever imagine hearing.

They decided to call the little thing "Gift from God", and they became attached to it with all their hearts.

They started to believe that the Great Architect of the Universe had finally forgiven them. Through the intercession of the angels in the skies above, they told the Creator that they wanted to have many more children like this.

The Greatest Force granted their wish.

Adam and Eve learnt how to laugh and smile from this little guest.

And from then on, whenever their children laughed, they would laugh too, and whenever their children cried, they could not hold back their tears either.

And from that day to this, mothers and fathers have behaved in the same way with their children as Adam and Eve learnt how to.

Whodunnit?

In the town of Ion, five children, all aged between eight and ten, were having a great time playing leapfrog on the plain near the coast in the south-facing grove when they found a body.

Three of them were girls, the other two were boys.

It was about ten in the morning and the event more than likely left the children deeply scarred psychologically. However, it is not the point of this story to go in to psychological analyses.

The body was that of a man in his forties. It was naked. The clothes were found scattered about thirty feet away from the body.

The children ran to the police station in the town, afraid, nauseous and tearful, and stammered out what they had seen to the police.

In that country, although violence had taken hold in many places, the town of Ion was not used to unusual events like this. It was somewhere where quiet and inoffensive people could live their lives in peace. And they were proud of it. Ever since the town had been founded – almost a century ago – no one had ever found any dead bodies, men or women.

The news spread quickly. TV cameras filmed what was happening. Whose body was it? Had he been murdered?

The investigation began. Detective Smith was charged with unravelling what had happened. Even if it turned out to be a Gordian knot, in his hands, it was bound to come undone. It was a murder and there were no clues. Mr Smith questioned everyone who he suspected.

The case was never solved. He ascertained who the body belonged to, but the murderer's identity never came to light.

Maybe it was something that the secret services had decided to end in their own subtle way.

What could Detective Smith do? Orders were orders and he had a wife and kids to think about.

Ataturk and the Young Child

November 10, 1938 Ankara, Yegen Bey District, alias the Jewish Quarter.

"Ataturk passed away!"

Her mother was washing the clothes, crouching over the washtub.

Upon hearing this word, his mother's body stiffened.

She hardly stood up; took her head between her two hands.

She looked towards the side where the voice came from.

Her aunt was at the vestibule. It was she who laid these words out.

Her mother asked with a shivering voice, "Did he die?"

The aunt nodded meaning "Yes," and began to cry.

Her mother also couldn't get hold of herself anymore. Tears dissolved

down her cheeks.

A few minutes later, mother's and father's mothers both entered through the street door.

They were sobbing too.

Maternal grandmother was asking herself and around: "What will we do now?"

None of the people there were able to answer this question.

A few more women among the neighbors piled into the yard. Faces of all were wet by tears.

The young child was three years old.

He would show his three fingers to those who ask his age and say three, three by word. It was because his father taught him so.

He dreams that night. This is an instance that he will never forget.

The picture in the living room comes to life while he sleeps soundly; the one his older sister said, "This is a picture of Ataturk." The handsome soldier in the picture smiles at him. He responds with a smile. He feels his face flushed by shame.

He would always remember their conversation with Ataturk throughout his lifetime:

Ataturk asks, "Are you okay?"

Encouraged by Ataturk's smile, he says, "I am cross with you!"

Ataturk's eyebrows slightly frown. "Why?" he asks. "What did I do to you!"

The child answers immediately. "Because you died. Now that you died,

my mother, my both grandmothers and the whole street cried. If you didn't die,

they would not cry either!"

Ataturk says, "Yes, you are right." "I shouldn't have died."

The child says "Please, don't die again! "Promise me, you will never die again."

"Well," says Ataturk. "If you don't want me to die, I won't die then."

Suddenly the child asks, "Do you have a child?"

"I do" says Ataturk.

"How many do you have?"

He says "Millions."

"How many are there in millions?"

Ataturk asks, "How high can you count?"

With pride, the child says, "I know how to count to five. Let me count.

1,2,3,4,5."

"Good job" says Ataturk. "You counted correctly."

The child persists, "How many are there in millions?"

Ataturk answers, "Many, many times five."

The child narrows both eyes slightly. It is apparent that he desires to reach millions.

However, upon understanding this is not as easy as he thought, as if to change the subject:

He asks, "Will you play with me?"

He becomes so happy to hear Ataturk telling, "Yes, I will play!"

Enthusiastically, the child says, "Look Atatürk," "Well I will sleep now, then

I will get up and then I will brush my teeth, because otherwise my mum shouts at me, then I will eat something, if I call you later, will you come?"

"I will come!"

The child looks at Ataturk with admiration. "I am my mother's child, my father's child, and may I also be your child?"

Ataturk says, "You may, I would love to!"

Upon this answer, the child spreads both arms wide, and cries out: "Ataturk, I love you so much!"

Ataturk spreads both arms wide, and says "My child, I love you so much too!"

The child walks towards Ataturk with arms wide open and they embrace one another.

The child suddenly sees himself as a teenager in the mirror.

Suddenly he sees himself with his hair turned grey,

And suddenly he sees his hair gone white.

Ataturk is always with him and with brightly shining smile in his eyes; he is constantly looking at him.

Harmful Books

The child in the fourth grade of elementary school tells his father excitedly when he is home from work in the evening; "Dad, the teacher wants to see you tomorrow. It is also written in this letter." His father reads the letter given by the child: "I ask you to come to the school to discuss a matter of issue about your child." The father scolds his son. Did you misbehave or do something naughty? The boy answers pretty naively: "No, I did not do anything bad." The father persists: How is school going? Did you get a bad mark? The child says: "My marks are either good or very good." The father asks, "Did you get in a fight with one of your friends?" The child answers: "I did not fight with anyone." The father says impatiently; "Oh son, if you haven't done any of these, why would the teacher want to see me?" The child says; "How should I know!" The next day, the father drives his car early in the morning. The school is either at the hill or in the valley of the city, at the end of nowhere, that is to say at a very difficult place. The roads were not built. Going up and down through the bumps, he arrives the range. He tells the name of the teacher to the guardsman and says that he wants to have a talk with her. The guardsman unwillingly calls the teacher from the phone over the desk. With an attitude as if he were making an explanation about a vital matter: Please wait awhile, the bell is going to ring.

You will meet the teacher when he gets out of the class. The father has a quick look around. The school is lacking many things. "Hopefully everything will work out all right.", he wholeheartedly wishes. The tone of the bell sounds like a sweet music to his ears. He is impatient, doubts if his son has a problem. He thinks that since they called him to the school, it must be important! A few minutes later, a thin, mignon young lady walks right towards him. The father says: "I wonder what the matter of issue is; since you called me it must me something important?" The teacher says; "Yes, it is important. Your son reads harmful books." The father says; "Harmful books? I haven't seen him reading harmful books at all. What does he read?" The teacher tells; "A lot of strip cartoon, picture books. Tommiks, Texsas, Zagor. Such things that I cannot even keep track of the names" The father asks; "How are his lessons? Does he follow you during the class? Or is he naughty?" The teacher tells; "His lessons are good, he likes to learn, he listens to what I am telling. He is a smart child. Yet, he should not read harmful books. Also he gives them to his friends." What would the father do? It was he who bought the strip cartoons. About two months ago, his son said to him "Dad" I like these strip cartoon, picture books very much. Every week they release twenty four kinds of those. Can we buy those? I would like to read them all." And the father said to him "Alright." They would leave the house together on Saturday mornings and always loaded the new releases from the same bookstore into the child's bag. And his son read the books one after another with great eagerness like he swallowed them. So the teacher called him for this. He was surprised. What sort of an explanation would he make? If he told something like "I bought the books to him, and I see no harm in his reading", an argument between him and the teacher could arise. And the passers-by would overhear it. This could undermine the teacher's authority among his colleagues. The teacher says; "Look, I am the teacher. And until now I have not ever read these books. My father would not allow me anyway." While telling this, she was in pride. The very young woman of the mercy of education. Should he smile or get angry? The teacher was criticizing him by saying, "My father would not allow me anyway." and was almost implying "You are not a good father!" He decided to cut his words short without more ado and said "I will talk with my son tonight." The teacher said, "Thanks for your interest."

On the evening of the same day, as soon as the child's father returned home from work, the child asked; "Dad, what did you do? Did you meet the teacher today?" He answered "Yes, she is complaining about you reading strip cartoon, picture books during break times. From now on you read these books at home. Also do not give them to your friends at school because they also need playing at break times. The child says, "Okay. The teacher is a little weird anyway. She does not like to read." A month later, one day the child said to his father: "Dad, I will not read strip cartoon, picture books anymore." The father asked "Why, are you fed up with it?" "You know what they are doing? They are changing the name of the book that they sold two months ago. These are always the same or too similar things. We also give a lot of money to them." "So, shouldn't we buy other books instead?" "You know hardcover children's books; Guliver's Travels, Andersen Tales or so. Let's buy some of those. "'Of course. It would be good."

At that moment, the father thought of the argument with his wife two months ago. His wife was definitely against buying strip cartoon, picture books to their son. He was able to soothe his wife by saying, "Let's wait awhile. He will get bored of strip cartoons and will read other things. And now he was seeing, he was right, he hit the mark. The child had reached a certain stage in three months and the old ones started not to satisfy him. He was looking for the better. A month later, children's classic books took the place. When his son started high school, the works of Steinbeck, Hemingway, Orhan Kemal and Sait Faik came into play. In addition to these, his lessons were good enough that he brought letter of thanks with each report card. Years later, on the evening of the day their son received his high school diploma, "Look" he said to his wife as he sipped his iced raki (strong turkish spirit flavored with anise), "let the child read whatever he reads. Reading habit and pleasure develops by it. Even books containing infamous sex stories should not be considered harmful." His wife laughed and said, "Why don't you tell me that plainly! In such books, there are items that even mothers and fathers might like."

What if I don't pay?

By the second year of the infants', he had long since got to the level where he could read with ease. He always had his head in one of those adventure stories written for children. He read the ones that were really exciting twice. And one of his greatest pleasures was to tell his friends every juicy detail about what happened in them.

One Monday morning as he was going to school, he saw a new bookshop. It must have opened on Sunday when he went to the forest with his friends; otherwise, he would definitely have noticed something as important as that.

He looked at his watch; he still had half an hour before the bell would ring.

He had just started to murmur the names of the books in the window to himself one by one when he noticed that he was being watched from the door by quite a tall man with thick hair and a sweet smile on his face who he later learnt was the owner of the shop.

"Don't you want to come inside? It'll be easier for you to look at the books."

He blushed. Even though his mother had told him time and time again that in situations like that he should say thank you, he did not. He was embarrassed.

He went into the shop and started to look over the shelves that were filled with books.

"Do you see anything you like? Look, over here it's only children's books."

Suddenly, at the end of one of the shelfs, he caught sight of volume two of *The Adventures of the Two Musicians*... Volume one had been so exciting. He gulped. Reluctantly, he pointed at a book and asked how much it was.

"Ten lira, but this is the second volume; just before you came in, a woman bought the first volume for her nephew."

On the cover of the book, there was the picture of the Two Musicians. He continued looking at it in awe.

The shopkeeper interrupted, "Do you know this book?"

The child looked up with pride and said, "I've read the first volume; this is the second."

"Well, buy it too and read it."

The boy was torn between saying and not saying:

"But it's very expensive; I don't have that much money."

The shopkeeper knew exactly how to talk to children.

"How much do you have?"

"Six lira."

"Have you saved it up from your pocket money?"

"Yes."

"And how much pocket money do you get?"

"Five lira."

"You really want this book, don't you?"

"Yes."

"Well, why don't we do something like this, then? Give me your six lira and you can pay the remaining four lira in two installments: two lira next week and two lira the week after... What do you say?"

The boy's was slowly coming to trust the shopkeeper more and more:

"That's what my mum does, too. Every week a woman comes round, and my mum gives her the money for the things she bought the month before. Every week just a little."

"And what does your mother buy?"

The boy blushed a little, but at the same time he did not want to leave the question unanswered.

"Oh, I don't know: things women wear."

The shopkeeper was starting to take more interest in this boy. He reminded him of his grandson.

"How old are you?"

"Seven. I'm in the second year of the infants'."

"Good for you! Now, let me do you a favour. Take the book, give me six lira now, and pay the rest over two weeks, OK?"

The boy opened his bag happily and carefully took out the money from a little envelope and handed it to the shopkeeper. As he was wrapping the book up, the shopkeeper could not help but notice that the boy seemed to be preoccupied. So he asked:

"What's wrong?"

"Aren't you going to get me to sign something?"

"Why should I get you to sign something?"

"Well, you don't know me or my mum or my dad. You don't even know where we live. What if I never come back here? What if I don't pay you back what I owe?"

"I'm sure you'll be back and you'll pay off what you owe."

"But that woman got my mum to sign something."

"Well, I don't think it's necessary."

"What if I'm a bad kid? My mum isn't a bad woman, but she still had to sign something."

The shopkeeper asked, "Aren't you going to be late for school?" The boy looked at his watch nervously. This time he was able to say thank you.

As he was running to school, he bemoaned the fact that he sometimes had no idea how grown-ups' minds worked.